The Mystery of Mrs. Kim

Stan Cullimore
Illustrated by Karin Littlewood

Rigby

"You're late!" shouted Charlotte.

Naomi came running up. She was red in the face and panting. "I'm sorry! I ran all the way!" she said.

"This is the third time this week. Mrs. Brown will kill us!" said Charlotte.

"I said I was sorry!" said Naomi. "Look, I've got an idea."

Charlotte sighed. "What is it this time?"

"Well, we could walk to school down Taylor Street," said Naomi. "It's quicker."

"No way!" said Charlotte. "All those big spooky houses look like something out of a horror movie."

"Don't be silly!" laughed Naomi. "They're just old houses."

"Well, they give me the creeps," said Charlotte.

Naomi looked at her watch. "Look, what are you more scared of, Mrs. Brown or Taylor Street?"

Charlotte laughed. "OK, OK!" she said, and the two girls started to walk along Taylor Street.

The row of big old houses seemed to go on forever. The houses were tall and very dark. Each one had fences along the front and shutters on the windows.

"Those houses really scare me," said Charlotte.

"They're not scary," said Naomi, "they're just old. You know Robert in our class? Well, he lives on Taylor Street."

But Charlotte wasn't listening. She had stopped suddenly and she looked very worried.

"What's the matter?" asked Naomi.

"Look!" said Charlotte. She pointed to a house with black shutters. There was an old lady standing behind the railings. She was dressed in black from head to toe. And she was standing perfectly still, as if she was waiting for something to happen.

"What's she doing?" said Naomi.

"She looks like she's staring right at us," whispered Charlotte.

"Right through us, you mean," said Naomi.

"Shhhhh! Keep your voice down," hissed Charlotte.

Naomi gulped. "Do you think she's listening to us?"

"I don't know, but I don't like this. I'm frightened," said Charlotte

"So am I," said Naomi. "Come on." She grabbed her friend's arm and ran.

Together they raced past the old lady and didn't stop until they got to the end of the street.

The next morning Naomi was late again. Charlotte was really angry this time.

"Come on!" she snapped, and they walked along the road without speaking.

They went up the hill and came to the corner of Taylor Street. They looked down the long row of houses. Then they looked at one another.

"This is silly," said Naomi.

"I don't know what you mean," said Charlotte.

"Oh come on, Charlotte, admit it! You're scared of that old lady, aren't you?"

"So are you!" snapped Charlotte. "Anyway, I just think we should go the usual way to school today, that's all."

"But we'll be late," said Naomi. "I think we should go down Taylor Street again."

"I don't know," said Charlotte, shaking her head.

"Come on, Charlotte, don't be a chicken!" urged Naomi. "I bet she won't even be there today."

"I'm not a chicken!" said Charlotte.

"OK, fine! Let's walk down Taylor Street again," said Naomi.

The girls walked quickly past the row of houses. When they got to the house with black shutters, the old lady was nowhere to be seen. Charlotte gave a sigh of relief.

"Told you so," said Naomi.

Both of them began to giggle, thinking about how scared they had been. Then, suddenly, the big, black door creaked open.

"Oh no!" said Charlotte.

"Wait!" shouted the old lady.

But the girls turned around, put their heads down, and ran as fast as they could.

They raced around the corner of the street and charged straight into Robert. Books and bags went flying.

"Hey! Watch where you're going!" cried Robert. "Have you two seen a ghost?"

"Er, no," said Naomi.

"But there's this old lady," said Charlotte.

Naomi pointed. "She lives in the house with black shutters."

Robert looked down the street. He nodded.

"I know her. That's Mrs. Kim. She's nice, isn't she?"

"Nice?" said Naomi. "She was staring at us! She's scary!"

"I don't think Mrs. Kim could have stared at you," Robert said.

"Why not?" asked Naomi.

"Because she's blind," said Robert.

"Blind?" The girls looked at each other, confused.

"Oh no!" said Charlotte. "I feel really stupid now."

"She must have thought we were really rude, running away like that," said Naomi.

"Look, why don't I take you to meet her tomorrow?" said Robert. "Then you can tell her you're sorry in person."

"I don't know," said Charlotte. She still looked scared.

"My big brother says it's best to face up to your fears," said Robert.

The girls looked at each other.

"OK," said Naomi. "We'll meet you here tomorrow, at quarter to nine."

The next morning, Naomi was on time! Robert and the two girls began to walk down the street, toward Mrs. Kim's house.

"So why does she stand behind the railings all the time?" asked Charlotte. "It's a little weird."

Robert shrugged. "She likes listening to the kids as they go by on their way to school."

Naomi frowned.

"She likes the company," said Robert. He kicked at a stone. "I think she gets lonely."

"How come you know so much about her?" asked Naomi.

"Because I always talk to her on my way to school," replied Robert. "She's amazing. She can tell it's me by the sound of my footsteps."

Mrs. Kim was waiting behind the fence of her house. Robert went up to her.

"Good morning, Robert," said Mrs. Kim.

The two girls gasped.

Robert laughed. "Hello, Mrs. Kim. I've brought some friends to meet you. This is Naomi and this is Charlotte."

"Good morning, it's great to meet you at last!" said Mrs. Kim. She laughed, and suddenly she didn't look scary at all.

Charlotte smiled. "Hello Mrs. Kim. It's great to meet you, too."

"Yes," said Naomi. "We're sorry we ran away."

"Come on," said Robert. "It's time to go to school."

Mrs. Kim nodded. "You're right. You had better get along. You mustn't be late."

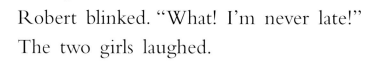

She smiled. "Girls, will you make sure that Robert gets to school on time?"

Robert blinked. "What! I'm never late!"

The two girls laughed.

21

After saying goodbye to Mrs. Kim, the three friends walked off, side by side.

"I feel bad about running away from Mrs. Kim the other day," said Naomi.

"So do I," said Charlotte. "But she did look a little scary."

Robert shrugged. "My big brother always says that you shouldn't judge people by the way they look."

22

"Your big brother says a lot of things,
doesn't he?" said Naomi.

"I think he's right," said Charlotte.

"So do I," admitted Naomi.

Robert grinned. "Well, don't tell him!
His head's big enough already!"

"I'm going to walk down Taylor Street every day now!" said Naomi.

"I bet you'll still be late," laughed Charlotte.